The Countries

India

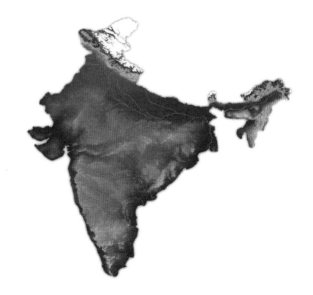

Bob Italia
ABDO Publishing Company

visit us at
www.abdopub.com

Published by ABDO Publishing Company, 4940 Viking Drive, Suite 622, Edina, Minnesota 55435. Copyright © 2002 by Abdo Consulting Group, Inc. International copyrights reserved in all countries. No part of this book may be reproduced in any form without written permission from the publisher.

Printed in the United States.

Photo Credits: Corbis
Art Direction & Maps: Neil Klinepier

Library of Congress Cataloging-in-Publication Data

Italia, Bob, 1955-
   India / Bob Italia.
     p. cm. -- (Countries)
   Includes index.
   Summary: Provides an overview of the history, geography, people, economy, government, and other aspects of life in India.
   ISBN 1-57765-752-7
    1. India--Juvenile literature. [1. India.] I. Title. II. Series.

DS407 .I85 2002
954--dc21

2001045855

Contents

Namaskar!

Hello from India! India has the second-largest population in the world. Only China has more people. India's capital is New Delhi. Mumbai is its largest city.

India is a land of great variety and contrast. The world's tallest mountains rise along its northern border. India also has deserts, plains, rivers, rain forests, and tropical lowlands. And it is home to a wide variety of plants and animals.

The people of India belong to many different **ethnic** groups and speak hundreds of dialects and languages. And they practice many religions. Every region of India has religious holidays and festivals.

Several ancient empires developed in India. In the late 1700s, India came under British rule. It did not win its independence until 1947.

India has a **parliamentary** system of government. Agriculture is the most important part of its **economy**. Its railway system provides most of the country's transportation.

Throughout the centuries, **architecture** and sculpture have played an important part in Indian **culture**. Today, the motion-picture industry is one of the country's leading art forms.

Namaskar *from India!*

Fast Facts

NEW DELHI

OFFICIAL NAME: Republic of India
CAPITAL: New Delhi

LAND
- Mountain Ranges: Himalaya, Satpura, Vindhya, Aravali, Eastern Ghats, Western Ghats
- Highest Peak: Kanchenjunga 28,208 feet (8,598 m)
- Major Rivers: Brahmaputra, Indus, Ganges

PEOPLE ✓
- Population: 57,092,000 (2002 est.)
- Major Cities: New Delhi, Delhi, Mumbai
- Language: Hindi
- Religions: Hindu, Islam, Christianity, Sikh

GOVERNMENT
- Form: Federal republic
- Head of State: President
- Head of Government: Prime minister
- Legislature: Parliament
- National Anthem: "Jana-gana-mana" ("Thou Art the Ruler of the Minds of All People")

ECONOMY
- Agricultural Products: Bananas, beans, chickpeas, coconuts, cotton, jute, mangoes, onions, oranges, peanuts, pepper, potatoes, rice, sesame seeds, sorghum, sugarcane, tea, wheat
- Manufactured Products: Bicycles, brassware and silverware, cement, chemicals, clothing and textiles, fertilizer, food products, iron and steel, jute bags and rope, leather goods, machinery, medicines, motor vehicles, paper, petroleum products, rugs, sewing machines, sugar, wood products
- Mining Products: Coal, iron ore, limestone, petroleum
- Money: Rupee (100 paise = 1 rupee)

India's flag

Indian rupees

Timeline

2500 B.C.	Civilization develops in the Indus Valley
1500	Aryans from central Asia come to India
500s to 400s	Buddhism and Jainism founded
324	Chandragupta Maurya forms the Mauryan Empire
A.D. 50	Kushans establish a dynasty
320 to 455	Gupta dynasty takes control of northern India
1498	Vasco da Gama arrives in Calcutta
1526	Mughal Empire established
1600	East India Company opens trade with India
mid-1700s	Mughal Empire ends
1774	Warren Hastings becomes the first governor general
1857	Rebellion spreads in India
1930	Mohandas K. Gandhi leads protest march
1947	Indian and British leaders divide the country into India and Pakistan; India gains independence; Jawaharlal Nehru becomes India's first prime minister
1966	Indira Gandhi becomes prime minister
1984	Indira Gandhi assassinated; Rajiv Gandhi becomes prime minister
1998	Atal Behari Vajpayee becomes prime minister; nuclear weapons tested
2000	Three new states form in India

History

People have lived in India for at least 200,000 years. About 4,500 years ago, a civilization developed in the Indus Valley. Then around 1500 B.C., Aryans from central Asia came to India.

In the 500s and 400s B.C., Siddhartha Gautama, who became known as Buddha, founded Buddhism, while Mahavira founded Jainism. Both religions spread rapidly throughout India.

Great Buddha at Bodh Gaya, India

About 324 B.C., Chandragupta Maurya formed the Mauryan Empire across northern India. The empire ended about 185 B.C. In the next 500 years, the Kushans from central Asia moved into northern India. They established their **dynasty** around A.D. 50.

The Gupta dynasty took control of northern India from about 320 to 455. Portuguese explorer Vasco da Gama arrived in Calcutta in 1498. He became the first European to reach India. Then India fell under the control of foreign invaders until the early 1500s.

A scene showing Babur at the spring of Khanja Sili Yaram in Kabul

In 1526, a central Asian leader named Babur established the Mughal Empire in India.

He ruled until 1530. Babur's grandson, Akbar, became the greatest Mughal emperor. He ruled from 1556 to 1605.

Akbar's grandson, Shah Jahan, ruled from 1628 to 1658. He built a new capital in Delhi, and constructed the Taj Mahal at Agra.

Governor General Warren Hastings

In 1600, England's East India Company opened trade with India and East Asia. It established trading posts and forts in a number of Indian cities.

By the mid-1700s, the Mughal Empire was at an end. The East India Company began seizing political power. In 1774, England's Warren Hastings became the first governor general of India.

In 1857, **rebellion** began to spread in India. A year later, Great Britain appointed a **viceroy** to govern India and stop the rebellion. The British retained control of India. But Indians still wanted their independence.

In 1930, Mohandas K. Gandhi led hundreds of Indians on a 240-mile (386-km) peaceful protest march. He also encouraged other peaceful acts of civil disobedience. The British decided

Mohandas K. Gandhi

to give the Indian people more political power.

In 1947, Indian and British leaders agreed to divide the country into India and Pakistan. India became an independent nation on August 15, 1947. Jawaharlal Nehru became the first **prime minister**. An **assembly** wrote a new **constitution**. It took effect on January 26, 1950. India held its first general elections in 1951 and 1952.

Nehru died in 1964. Lal Bahadur Shastri became **prime minister**. Then in 1966, Indira Gandhi, Nehru's daughter, became prime minister. She was **assassinated** on October 31, 1984. Her son, Rajiv Gandhi, became prime minister. But he was accused of **corruption**. In 1989, he resigned. A **coalition** of political parties formed a new government. While campaigning for the 1991 elections, Rajiv Gandhi was assassinated.

P. V. Narasimha Rao won the election and became prime minister. Rao worked to reduce government control of the **economy**.

In 1998, Atal Behari Vajpayee became prime minister. In May, India tested its first **nuclear** weapons. This created much tension in the region. In response, Pakistan developed its own nuclear weapons.

In 2000, the government formed the three new states of Jharkhand, Uttaranchal, and Chhattisgarh. India also renamed several of its major cities. Bombay became Mumbai, Calcutta was renamed Kolkata, and Madras is now called Chennai.

India faced many political problems in the new century. Conflicts between Hindus and Muslims increased as Hindu nationalists attempted to make India a Hindu state. Tensions with Pakistan remained, while the Punjab, Assam, and Jammu and Kashmir regions struggled for more independence.

Atal Behari Vajpayee

The Land

India has three main land regions. The regions are the Himalaya, the Northern Plains, and the Deccan or Southern **Plateau**.

The Himalaya is the world's highest mountain range. Many of its mountain peaks are covered with snow throughout the year. India's tallest mountain peak, Kanchenjunga, is in this region.

The Northern Plains stretch across northern India. The Brahmaputra, Indus, and Ganges Rivers flow through this region, so the soil is fertile and excellent for farming. The Thar Desert is in the western part of the Plains.

The Deccan Plateau makes up most of India's southern **peninsula**. The Satpura, Vindhya, and Aravali mountain ranges separate it from the Northern Plains. On the eastern edge of the Deccan lies a rugged mountain range called the Eastern Ghats. The Western Ghats run along the western edge.

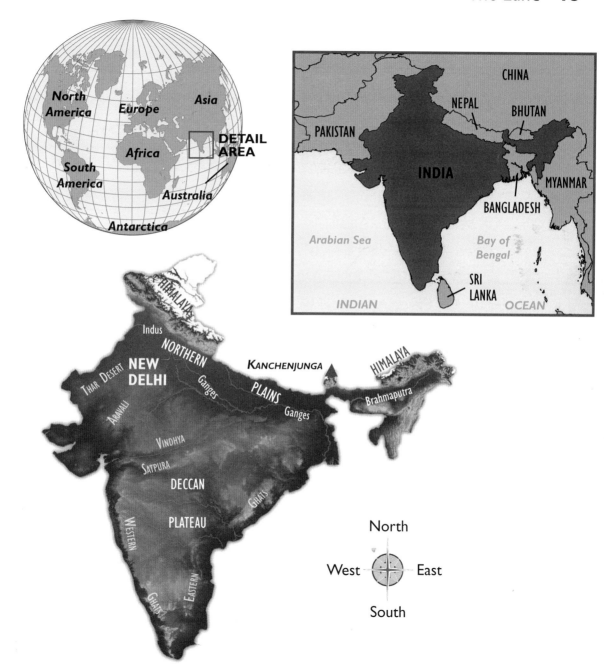

DETAIL AREA

North America
Europe
Asia
Africa
South America
Australia
Antarctica

CHINA
NEPAL
BHUTAN
PAKISTAN
INDIA
MYANMAR
BANGLADESH
Arabian Sea
Bay of Bengal
SRI LANKA
INDIAN OCEAN

HIMALAYA
Indus
NORTHERN
NEW DELHI
THAR DESERT
KANCHENJUNGA
PLAINS
HIMALAYA
Ganges
Ganges
Brahmaputra
ARAVALI
VINDHYA
SATPURA
DECCAN
GHATS
PLATEAU
WESTERN GHATS
EASTERN GHATS

North
West — East
South

India has three main weather seasons. The cool season lasts from October to February. The hot season lasts from March to June. The rainy season usually lasts from June to September.

During the rainy season, winds called monsoons blow from the Indian Ocean. The monsoons bring steady, heavy rains, and often cause much flood damage.

People are caught in the monsoon rain in Simla, India.

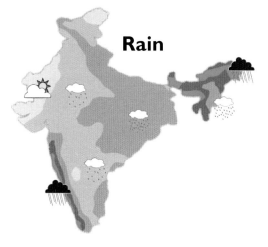

Rain

Rainfall

AVERAGE YEARLY RAINFALL

Inches		Centimeters
Under 20		Under 50
20 - 40		50 - 100
40 - 80		100 - 200
80 - 120		200 - 300
Over 120		Over 300

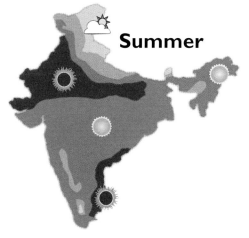

Summer

Temperature

AVERAGE TEMPERATURE

Fahrenheit		Celsius
Over 85°		Over 29°
75° - 85°		24° - 29°
65° - 75°		18° - 24°
55° - 65°		13° - 18°
45° - 55°		7° - 13°
Below 45°		Below 7°

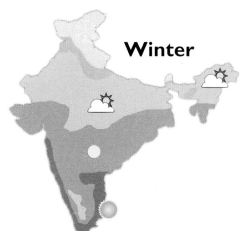

Winter

Plants & Animals

India has a wide variety of plants and animals. Tropical evergreen forests grow in rainy areas. **Deciduous** forests, scrubs, grasslands, and desert vegetation are found in drier climates. **Coniferous** forests grow in the Himalaya. Teak trees grow on the **peninsula**. Palm trees are found in the tropical regions. Sal, sandalwood, rosewood, and more than ten thousand other kinds of flowering plants also grow in India.

India is home to some of the world's largest animals. The foothills of the Himalaya are home to many kinds of wildlife, including tigers, snow leopards, deer, and rhinoceroses. Elephants and monkeys are found in the Eastern and Western Ghats.

Thousands of different kinds of birds are found in India, including herons, peacocks, storks, cranes, ibis, and flamingos. India's birds of prey include hawks, vultures, and eagles.

There are almost 400 kinds of snakes in India. Kraits and cobras are the most poisonous species. The Indian python lives in marshy areas and grasslands. Turtles and lizards are found throughout the country. Crocodiles live in its rivers, swamps, and lakes.

An Indian rhinoceros

Indians

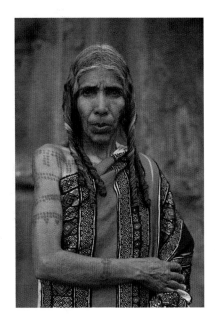

A Dravidian woman in traditional dress

India's two main **ethnic** groups are the Dravidians and the Indo-Aryans. Most Dravidians live in the south, while most Indo-Aryans live in the north. Many smaller groups such as the Bhils, Gonds, Khasis, Mizos, Mundas, Oraons, and Santals live in India's remote areas.

More than 1,000 languages and dialects are spoken in India. India's national language is Hindi, which is taught in public schools.

Most Indians work as farmers and live in villages made up of mud-and-straw houses. The homes usually have one or two rooms with mud floors. Wealthier families live in brick or concrete houses.

Indians are organized into four main social groups called **castes**. The highest caste, the Brahmans, are priests and scholars. The Kshatriyas are rulers and warriors. The Vaishyas are merchants and professionals, while the Shudras are **artisans**, laborers, and servants. Those outside the caste system are called untouchables. They hold the most undesirable jobs, such as garbage disposal.

An Indian woman from the Brahmin caste

India has no official religion, but the people practice many faiths. Most Indians are Hindus. Some are Muslims. The smallest religious groups include Buddhists, Christians, Jains, and Sikhs.

A member of the untouchable caste

A young woman in a sari

Indians wear a variety of clothing types, depending on their region, religion, or **ethnic** group. Loose clothing is popular because of India's tropical climate. The most common article of clothing for women is the *sari*. Many men wear *dhotis*.

Rice and wheat are the main foods of India. **Pulses**, chickpeas, and lentils are also popular. Most Indian meals are cooked in **ghee** or vegetable oil. Indian food is often spiced with coriander, cumin, garlic, ginger, mustard seeds, red pepper, or turmeric. Tea is the most popular beverage.

Temple musicians wearing dhotis

The Hindu faith forbids its followers to eat beef, while Muslims cannot eat pork. So many Indians are vegetarians.

Children from age 6 through 14 receive free education. But only half of the children over age 10 continue their education. About half of the population cannot read or write.

Primary school children learn to read and write Hindi.

A Rabari woman makes chapati in her simple kitchen. She wears traditional silver armbands, an embroidered choli, and a black shawl with red dots distinctive of her tribe.

Chapati

Whole Wheat Flatbread

2 1/4 cups durum flour
1/2 teaspoon sea salt

1 tablespoon canola oil
2/3 cup very warm water

Combine flour and salt in a large mixing bowl. Mix in oil and water to form a stiff dough, adding more water if needed. Remove dough from bowl and knead on a lightly floured surface until smooth, about 5 minutes. Return dough to bowl, cover with a towel and set aside in a warm place for one hour. Place dough onto a lightly floured surface and divide into 14 equal portions.

Roll each portion into a ball and cover them with a damp towel. Heat an ungreased griddle or large frying pan over medium heat. Working with one ball of dough at a time, flatten it, then roll into a 6-inch circle. When griddle is hot, pick up dough, shake off extra flour and place it on the hot pan. Cook until brown spots appear, about one minute. Flip dough over and cook on other side. Cover and place in a warm oven while cooking remaining chapatis.

AN IMPORTANT NOTE TO THE CHEF: Always have an adult help with the preparation and cooking of food. Never use kitchen utensils or appliances without adult permission and supervision.

English	Hindi
Boy _____	Larka
Girl _____	Larki
Hello _____	Namaskar
Father _____	Bap
Mother _____	Ma
Thank you _____	Dhanya-waadh

LANGUAGE

The Economy

Agriculture is the most important part of India's **economy**. India is the world's leading producer of cauliflower, jute, mangoes, millet, **pulses**, sesame seeds, and tea. Indians grow grains such as rice, wheat, and corn. They also grow bananas, cabbages, coconuts, coffee, cotton, onions, oranges, peanuts, potatoes, rapeseeds, rubber, sugarcane, and tobacco. Spices such as cardamom, ginger, pepper, and turmeric are also important products.

India has more cattle than any other country. The cows are used for plowing and to make dairy products such as milk and butter. Cattle hides are used to make leather goods.

India is one of the world's leading iron- and steelmakers. Indian factories make aircraft, automobiles, bicycles, electrical appliances, military equipment, railway cars, sewing machines, and tractors.

Manufacturers also make cement, medicines, dyes, fertilizer, food products, industrial chemicals, paper, **pesticides**, **petroleum** products, **textiles**, and wood products.

India has many natural resources. Iron ore, coal, diamonds, emeralds, gold, and silver are its important mining products. People who live on India's coasts often fish for a living.

Petroleum and coal are used to produce most of India's electric power. The rest comes from **hydroelectric** power plants.

Cattle graze near an irrigated rice field.

Cities

New Delhi is the capital of India. It was built in the early 1900s, to replace Delhi as India's capital. New Delhi has gardens, parks, and wide streets. Government buildings, including **Parliament** House, are in the center of the city. Most people who live there work for the government. The city has no factories.

Mumbai is India's largest city. This city is a major financial center. It has many banks and insurance companies. Mumbai's factories make cotton **textiles**, leather, and railroad equipment. Most of the city's hotels, museums, schools, and theaters are in the old section of Mumbai.

Delhi is the second-largest city in India. It is also a center of finance. Delhi's factories make electrical machinery and equipment, metal products, and rubber.

Delhi has many important monuments, including the Red Fort, built by the Mughal Emperor Shah Jahan. But Delhi is also a crowded city with slums and narrow streets.

The parliament buildings in New Delhi

Transportation & Communication

Trains are the most important means of transportation in India. Its government-owned railway system is one of the largest in the world. Railroads transport most goods and passengers in India.

India has an extensive road system, but the roads are not well maintained. Buses are among the most popular forms of road transportation, especially in cities. Few Indians own automobiles. But motorcycle ownership is increasing.

In rural areas, many people travel on horse-drawn buggies or carts. Most major rivers carry boat traffic.

Air India is one of two government-owned airlines. It flies to many countries throughout the world. Indian Airlines flies within India and to nearby countries.

Major airports are found in Kolkata, Chennai, Delhi, Mumbai, and Trivandrum.

India has telephone and telegraph services. But few families have telephones. So people often use public telephones to make calls.

Radio stations provide news for most Indians. But even the poorest villages with electric power have at least one television set, which the people can view. Cable and satellite systems are becoming more common. India also has about 3,500 daily, privately-owned newspapers. They are published in a many different languages.

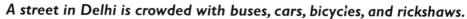
A street in Delhi is crowded with buses, cars, bicycles, and rickshaws.

Government

India is a **republic**. It has 28 states and 7 territories. India has a **parliamentary** system of government. India's parliament has two houses, the Lok Sabha and the Rajya Sabha. The parliament makes India's laws and elects India's president.

India's president is the head of state. He or she is elected by the parliament to a five-year term. The president signs parliamentary bills into law, and chooses the **prime minister**.

The prime minister heads the government. The prime minister also heads the Council of Ministers. The Council helps run the day-to-day government operations.

A council of elected elders, called a *panchayat*, governs most villages. The *panchayat* settles disagreements and hands out punishments.

An all-party meeting at Parliament House in New Delhi

Holidays & Festivals

Every region of India has its own religious holidays and festivals. One of the most popular religious festivals is Vasantpanchami, held in February. It honors Sarasvati, the Hindu goddess of learning and the arts.

Holi is a Hindu spring festival celebrated in February or March. People throw colored water and powder at one another. The usual **caste** restrictions are disregarded during this festival. The Dolayatra celebration takes place during Holi. People place images of the Hindu gods on decorated platforms. Then they swing the platforms to the accompaniment of special songs.

Indians celebrate Dussehra in September or October. People reenact the story of the Ramayana, celebrating the victory of Rama over the evil Ravana.

Hindus celebrate Diwali in October or November. It is a festival of lights devoted to Laksmi, the goddess of wealth. This festival is a time for lamplighting and exchanging gifts.

India has two major nonreligious holidays. Independence Day, on August 15, celebrates India's independence from Great Britain. **Republic** Day, on January 26, is India's great national festival. It celebrates the **constitution** of 1950.

The Holi festival celebrates the start of spring.

Sports & Leisure

Cricket is India's most popular sport. Indians also enjoy field hockey and soccer. Cards, chess, and kite flying are common recreational activities. Indians also enjoy watching television and movies. Attending concerts and plays is popular in large cities.

Architecture and sculpture have played an important part in Indian **culture**. They flourished during the Indus Valley civilization, about 2500 B.C. Hindu temples are famous for their design and sculptures. Ruins of Buddhist monasteries and **stupas** are popular tourist attractions.

The most famous building in India is the Taj Mahal in Agra. The Emperor Shah Jahan, a Muslim, built the Taj Mahal as a tomb for his favorite wife.

India is well-known for its fables and **folk tales**, including the Panchatantra, India's oldest collection.

Indian music has a sound all its own, because it uses **unique** stringed instruments like the sitar, sarod, and vina. India has several major styles of classical dance, including the *bharata natyam* and the *kathak*.

The earliest Indian written works, the Vedas, are about 3,000 years old. India's best-known modern writers are R. K. Narayan and Salman Rushdie. Each year, India's motion-picture industry makes hundreds of films in many languages.

The Taj Mahal

Glossary

architecture - the art of planning and designing buildings.

artisan - a person skilled in a craft or trade.

assassinate - to murder a very important person.

assembly - a group of people that make decisions.

caste - a social class based on wealth, profession, or occupation.

coalition - a group formed of different peoples, states, or classes.

coniferous - trees or shrubs that produce cones and do not lose their needles. Evergreen or pine trees are conifers.

constitution - the laws that govern a country.

corrupt - to be influenced by other people to be dishonest.

culture - the customs, arts, and tools of a nation or people at a certain time.

deciduous - trees that lose their leaves in the fall.

dynasty - a series of rulers who belong to the same family.

economy - the way a country uses its money, goods, and natural resources.

ethnic - a way to describe a group of people who have the same race, nationality, or culture.

folk tales - stories that are part of the beliefs, traditions, and customs of a people. Folk tales are handed down from parent to child.

ghee - purified butter.

hydroelectricity - the kind of electricity produced by water-powered generators.

nuclear - of or relating to atomic energy.

parliament - the highest lawmaking body of some governments.

peninsula - land that sticks out into water and is connected to a larger land mass.

pesticide - a chemical used to kill insects.

petroleum - a thick, yellowish-black oil. It is the source of gasoline.

plateau - a raised area of flat land.

prime minister - the highest-ranked member of some governments.

pulses - the edible seeds of peas, beans, lentils, and similar plants that have pods.

rebel - to disobey an authority or the government.

republic - a form of government in which authority rests with voting citizens and is carried out by elected officials such as parliament.

stupa - a dome-shaped structure, usually a Buddhist shrine.

textile - of or having to do with the designing, manufacturing, or producing of woven fabrics.

unique - unlike anything else.

viceroy - a governor who acts as the representative of a king or queen.

Web Sites

Indian Parliament
http://alfa.nic.in/
Step inside India's parliament at this informational site. Readers can visit each house, learn about the government, meet parliament members, and much more!

Indian Embassy
http://www.indianembassy.org
Get up-to-date information about India from the Indian Embassy in Washington, D.C. Readers can view news stories, press releases, and much more!

These sites are subject to change. Go to your favorite search engine and type in India for more sites.

Index